This igloo book belongs to:

....

igloobooks

Published in 2014
by Igloo Books Ltd
Cottage Farm
Sywell
NN6 0BJ
www.igloobooks.com

Copyright © 2014 Igloo Books Ltd

HUN001 1114
2 4 6 8 10 9 7 5 3 1
ISBN 978-1-78343-588-3

Written by Melanie Joyce
Illustrated by Kirsten Collier

Printed and manufactured in China

Kirsten
Collier

The Great
Chicken
Mystery

Melanie
Joyce

igloobooks

It was morning on Bluebell Farm
and Farmer Bob was up at dawn.
"I'll have eggs for breakfast," he said,
stretching and giving a yawn.

The hens were in the hen house.
Farmer Bob counted **twenty-four**.

"Hang on a minute," he said.
"I'm sure there should be two more."

"I've got twenty-**six** hens," said Bob.
"I'm missing my best two.
Someone's stealing my chickens...

... I'm going to find out **who!**"

Farmer Bob looked all around.
He saw **Foxy** sneaking by.

He looked a bit suspicious.
Farmer Bob wanted to find out why.

Foxy looked very sheepish.
"I don't **like** chicken," he said.
"I've become a vegetarian.
Now I eat blueberries instead."

"I must clear my name," said Foxy,
" or it will be curtains for me.

I'll wait until night and stay out of sight,
then see what I can see."

That night, Foxy crept into the coop,
carefully sniffing the ground.
He clicked on his detective torch
and shone it all around.

At first, everything was quiet.
Then, he saw...

... chickens

in the light.

"So **that's** what you are up to!" he said.
"You plan to escape tonight!"

The chickens clucked and flapped,
then promptly slammed the door.

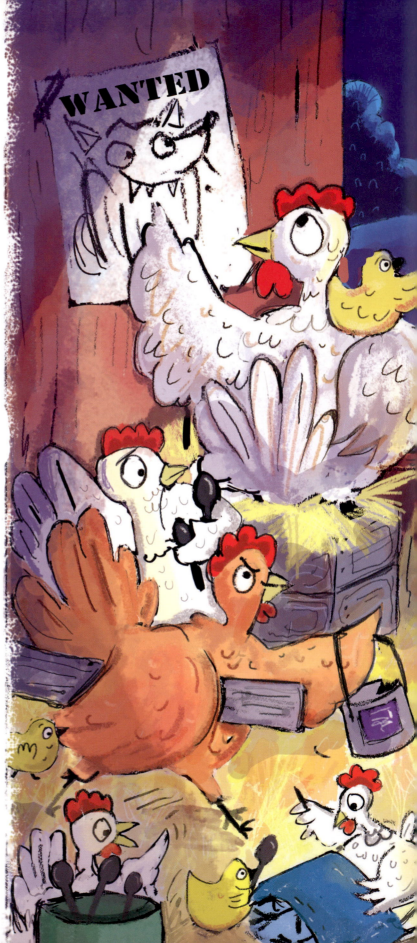

"Two of you got away," said Foxy,
"but there won't be any more."

"Those birds are simply brainless," thought Foxy. "They're daft and have no sense."

Meanwhile, the hens were hatching **a plan** to make it over the fence.

The hens dug and shovelled.
They built trampolines.
They used every trick they knew.

They clucked and flapped.

"Wey-hey!" they squawked...

...and over Foxy's head they flew.

"I'll catch you," said Foxy, crossly and he tried to set up a trap.

Those clever hens cut a hole in the fence...

... and crept out through the gap.

Foxy chased after those chickens
like he'd never chased them before.

"Got you!" he cried, with a dive,
wrestling one to the floor.

"What's going on?"
said a voice.
It belonged to Farmer Bob.
Foxy quivered with fear.
"Nothing," he said with a sob.

"I knew it was you," said Bob.
"I'll put you in a stew.
I'll cover you with pastry.
Then, it will be the oven for you."

Suddenly, there was lots of clucking.
There were chickens
everywhere.

"Please don't cook Foxy," they said in a flap.
"It really wouldn't be fair."

The cockerel explained that they'd
run away to find a **bigger** home.
"We want somewhere to peck and scratch,
where our little chicks can roam."

"Don't leave," said Bob.
"I'll build you a home. I'll get started right away.
It will be so much bigger and better. I'll finish it today."

The new hen house was **fantastic**.

There was a brand new chicken run.

Everyone helped to decorate it.

Even Foxy had some fun.

The hen house was a home that everyone adored.
Foxy was happy because his reputation was restored.
The flock of chickens grew and no one came to harm.
It was a happy ending for everyone on Bluebell Farm.